Dear Parents,

A love of reading is something we wish for every child. This book series is designed to encourage reading—with entry points appropriate to most any reader. Our well-defined levels help you choose books that are best suited to your child's interests and ability. These colorful books tap into a child's imagination and build confidence for a lifelong love of reading.

Our Read Smart bookmarks reinforce your child's reading vocabulary through games and activities. Take the time to make reading more fun by following the simple instructions on the bookmark.

Reading is a voyage that can take your child into wonderful, enchanting places. We are delighted to join you on this journey.

 **BEGINNING READER**

For children who are ready to read their first books, know their letter sounds, and have developed an understanding of early phonics skills. Words include short vowels, simple plurals, and sight words.

 DEVELOPING READER

For children who are ready for longer sentences and more lines of print per page. Stories are richer and include a growing vocabulary. Words feature beginning consonant blends.

 **CONFIDENT READER**

For children who are ready for books with longer sentences and richer plots. Words are longer and feature ending consonant blends and simple suffixes.

 ADVANCED READER

For children who are ready for books with more complex plots, varied sentence structure, and full paragraphs. Words feature long vowels and vowel combinations.

ISBN 1-60143-475-8

Pop Pop Pop!

Written by **Paige Russell**
Illustrated by **Shawn Finley**

I am Pig Wig.

I am Cat.

It's popcorn day.

We like that.

Pick up a pan.

Fill it to the top.

It gets hot.

Pop pop pop!

I like it hot.

Fill the bag to the top.

We eat it up.

Pop pop pop!

Yum yum yum!

Do you want more too?

Let's pop more for me and you.

Yum yum yum!

We want more.

Let's go to the popcorn store.

Tap tap tap.

Go in the shop.

We want popcorn!

Pop pop pop!

We see bags up on top.

We want popcorn!

Pop pop pop!

Go up up up.

We like this store.

We eat it up,

but we want more!

Get the box.

Tip the top.

Fill it up.

Pop pop pop!

That's too much.

It will not stop.

On and on and
pop pop pop!

It will fill the popcorn store.

It's up to my socks.

It will not stop.

It's up to my hips.

Pop pop pop!

It's up to my neck.

It's up to my hat.

Where is Pig Wig?

Where is Cat?

I like the smell.

What's in the shop?

Open up and . . .

Pop pop—

Pop!